Sunny
Goes to School

Written by Detta Juusola
Illustrated by Lavona Keskey

Woofspun Publishing
Maple Plain, Minnesota

Thank you...

Tami and Sharon Grabill of TLG Classy Canine, Long Lake, Minnesota. Your willingness to help, both in dog training and in producing this book, is very much appreciated. Congratulations, Tami, for receiving the 1994 Service Award Certificate of Commendation from Minnesota Governor Arne Carlson in recognition of your service to the community.

and thank you, Wendy Berglund, Sunny's breeder; Kim Dearth, Dog World Magazine; Susan Hauge, Twin City Training Center; Virginia Matanic, Wright County Kennel Club; Peggy Burnet, the Bookcase; Bill, Marla, Logan, and Jessie Juusola; Diane Feyo; LaDonn Peterson; Lois Siljander; Bonnie Fredrickson; and all who read the manuscript, answered questions, and offered suggestions and support.

DJ

Woofspun Publishing
P.O. Box 452
Maple Plain, MN 55359-0452
Phone (612) 479-2886
Fax (612) 479-1982

Editor: Jacqueline Reina
Cover design: Kathi Hillukka

10 9 8 7 6 5 4 3 2 1

Printed in the USA by Image Group International

Publisher's Cataloging in Publication
(Prepared by Quality Books Inc.)

Juusola, Detta.
    Sunny goes to school / written by Detta Juusola ; illustrated by
Lavona Keskey.
    p. cm.
    SUMMARY: Shows how Sunny and his handler, Marla, work together
to successfully complete a basic obedience course. Basic dog
obedience guidelines follow the story.
    ISBN 0-9639736-3-0

1. Dogs--Training--Fiction. I. Title.

PZ7.J887Sun 1996   [Fic]
                                     QBI95-20611

to Trent and K.C.

"Hey Marla! Let's call our new puppy Sunny," my little brother sang out. "Sunny Sunny Sunshine!"

It was cold outside, but our house was warm and full of smiling faces. We had waited a long time to get a Golden Retriever, and now he was really here.

Sunny fit right in with the family, just like he
belonged with my brothers and sisters and me.
Mom treated him like he was a new baby. Dad?
Well, he said we didn't need another dog, but
his twinkling eyes told me he liked Sunny as
much as the rest of us did.

"Sunny, you are the cutest puppy I've ever seen!" I giggled, as he tickled my cheek with a wet puppy kiss. And he really was! His golden fur was fluffy and soft, and his chocolate-brown eyes were warm and trusting. He scampered around the house on short, chubby legs, sniffing things with his little black nose.

"Look at the size of those feet!" exclaimed my dad as we watched Sunny climb onto my little brother's lap. "He's going to be one big dog."

A new puppy is kind of like a new baby. I
rocked Sunny to sleep the first night he was
home so that he wouldn't cry. Then I gently put
him in his bed without waking him.

Before we brought Sunny home, Mom had gone shopping to buy him some special things. He had his own blanket and a brand new cage that looked like a little house. He had a bone and some toys. He had lots of things. But best of all, he had people who loved him.

Sunny got bigger every day. I didn't know a
puppy could grow so fast. I didn't know how
much trouble he could get into either!

As the weeks went by, I tried to teach him
things a dog should know. He learned not to
bite at people with his sharp puppy teeth, and
he quit trying to steal food from my little
brother. He seemed to catch on pretty fast.
But not when it came to socks!

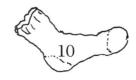

I don't know why Sunny loved socks so much.
No matter where we put our socks, that puppy
would find them and take them. He didn't care
if they were dirty or clean. He would run
through the house with socks hanging from his
mouth, and if nobody took them away, he would
chew holes in them.

Sunny always seemed to be around when I took off my socks. He'd wait right next to me, ready to grab them and run.

"Sunny, it's a good thing you're so cute. . . Sunny, NO! They're *my* socks!"

Sunny's eyes had a mischievous gleam as he
bounded away, my socks held firmly in his
mouth. The bigger he got, the harder he was to
catch. I didn't know what I was going to do with
him.

One morning I was lying in bed when my little
brother came running into my room shouting,
"Marla! Marla! Sunny Sunshine is on the table!"
I jumped up and ran into the kitchen.

Sunny was walking around on top of the table.
He carefully picked up a pair of socks from a
stack of clean folded clothes. He didn't look at
all guilty when he saw me watching him.
Actually, he looked rather proud of himself.

Sunny was a smart dog and a fast learner. I couldn't understand why sometimes he'd ignore me. Other times he'd respond right away. I began to notice that if he wanted something, he would obey me. But if he didn't want anything, he'd act like I wasn't around.

"Who's the boss here, anyway?" I asked myself.

One day Mom said, "Marla, I think we should take Sunny to school."

School? For a dog? I knew dogs needed to learn, but I thought only people went to school.

"I registered Sunny in a beginning obedience class," Mom continued. "Sunny will learn how to get along with other dogs, and we will learn how to teach him to obey."

Hm-m-m. Sunny obeying us *all* the time? That didn't sound bad.

"You spend a lot of time with him," she added. "Why don't you be his handler?"

I didn't know what a handler was supposed to do, but it sounded important and fun. I said, "Sure!"

The first day of school came quickly. I held tightly onto Sunny's leash as Mom and I walked down the stairs to the school.

What confusion! There were dogs and people everywhere! Dogs were pulling, jumping, and barking.

As the owners took their turns checking in with the teacher at the counter, they tried to keep their dogs under control. Soon it was our turn.

"Where is the Golden Retriever?" shouted the teacher over all the noise. Then she looked down at Sunny. "Oh, there he is! I see you need a training collar and different leash for him."

The teacher tried collars on Sunny until she found one that fit just right. Then she handed me a six-foot leather leash. "Now you have the equipment you'll be using during the course."

I clipped the leash onto Sunny's collar and looked around.

This wasn't at all like my school. It didn't look like a schoolroom at all. Two trails of rubber mats on the floor followed the walls of the big room. That's where we would work with our dogs.

The room was noisy. The owners tried to keep their dogs quiet and still, but the dogs barked and wanted to play. These dogs needed to learn to behave!

Mom and I sat down on two of the chairs that were lined up against a wall in the room and waited for class to start.

Sunny looked worried as he sat close by my feet. I was worried too. The other handlers were grown-ups. I was only 12 years old.

"Mom, maybe you should handle Sunny," I whispered.

"No," she answered, "you'll do just fine. Sunny would rather be with you."

"Hello! My name is Tami, and I'm your instructor. Welcome to our Beginning Obedience Class!"

I looked up. The teacher was standing in front of the class.

"Well, this is it," I thought. "Here goes."

"You might find this hard to believe," our teacher continued, "but by the time we finish our eight weeks of training, your dogs will be sitting quietly beside you. You will even be able to leave them lined up on one side of the room while you walk across to the other side."

Mom and I looked at each other in astonishment. Some dogs were really misbehaving. How would they ever learn anything, I wondered.

A lady with a cute little Cocker Spaniel was sitting a few chairs away from us. After the other dogs had settled down, this one kept barking and pulling at his leash. The teacher was trying to talk, but that dog's owner could not make him sit quietly. Finally, the teacher said, "Why don't you take your dog to the end of the row and face him away from the other dogs?"

The owner's face got all red, but she turned her dog so he couldn't see us and he was quiet after that.

The teacher continued. "A trained dog is a happy dog. A trained dog makes life more enjoyable for the people around him. Just as a child learns from practice, a dog learns by repeating too. In this class, we will train you how to train your dog."

"Train me?" I thought.

"You will have homework to do every day," the teacher explained. "You and your dog must practice the class lessons if you expect your dog to learn to obey you."

Wow! Both Sunny and I were going to have to do homework. This was going to be harder than I thought.

"Here comes Dustin," the teacher said, motioning toward a prancing Shetland Sheepdog who had just entered the room with a teaching assistant. "He's been through lots of training. If you work hard, your dog will learn to obey as well as Dustin does."

I watched carefully as the teaching assistant demonstrated how well Dustin obeyed her commands.

"Will Sunny be able to learn so well?" I wondered.

Then class began. "Dogs and handlers! On the floor!"

Before the teacher could give the first instructions, do you know what that little Cocker Spaniel did? The lady who owned him was so embarrassed. While the whole class waited, she had to get some sawdust and clean up after him!

First the teaching assistant and her Shetland Sheepdog demonstrated the "heel" command. The assistant walked. She ran. She turned. She stopped. No matter what she did, there was Dustin at her left side with his head next to her knee.

When we started practicing, Sunny acted a little confused. He looked at me with eyes that seemed to say, "I don't understand what you want me to do." But we kept working, and soon he began to stay close by my left side.

It wasn't long before Sunny was trotting happily alongside me without pulling and jerking on his leash. "Good dog, Sunny!"

When another dog came close to us, Sunny wanted to play. I had to remind him that he needed to pay attention to me. "Sunny, heel!"

Each time Sunny did something right, I'd tell him, "Good dog!" Our teacher kept reminding us that our dogs need lots and lots of praise.

Sunny tried hard to please me while we were working at school. But he liked our breaks too. Whenever our teacher called, "Exercise finished!" we quit working for a few minutes to relax and play.

I knew that Sunny was enjoying school. His big tail wagged so hard it made his whole body wiggle!

We went to school once a week. At each class we learned new things, and every day at home Sunny and I practiced our lessons.

"Sunny, sit." "Good dog!" "Down." "Good boy, Sunny!" "Sunny, no! " "Stay." "Good dog!" "Heel." "Sunny, come!" "Good dog!"

We practiced the commands over and over.

"It is very important that you practice at least a
short time every day," our teacher told us.

Sometimes it was hard to find the time to do
homework with Sunny because I had homework
from my school too.   But when we started
working, Sunny and I had so much fun together.

40

Sunny's class had lots of dogs in it, and each dog was different. Some dogs were bouncy and quick, and found it easy to follow commands like "sit."

Sunny found commands like "down" much easier.

Funny things happened at school too.

One day the Cocker Spaniel got away from his owner. As the teacher was explaining what we were going to do next, a small dog trotted up to her and sat down at her feet, his head cocked jauntily to one side.

The teacher looked down and said, "Somebody lost her dog!"

"Oh-h-h!" said the lady when she realized she had no dog at the end of her leash. That lady sure had a lot of trouble with her dog!

One day the teacher said, "Your dog needs to learn that he must obey you even when he is distracted by other things. 'Sit' your dogs. Your dogs will remain sitting and will be quiet. There will be no barking." I wondered what would happen next.

The teacher walked to the corner of the room and put her hand on something. A doorbell rang!

Dogs forgot all about sitting! Some dogs started barking! "STAY!" I commanded. Sunny jumped a little and looked around at all the confusion, but he didn't get up or bark.

"Good dog, Sunny!" I told him as I patted him on the head. Making Sunny stay while someone rang a doorbell was one of our homework exercises. Practice really works!

Not everybody finishes dog obedience school.
That lady with the Cocker Spaniel sure had a
hard time.

One day her dog wanted to play instead of
learn. The lady became so upset that she
picked him up and left and never came back.

"Don't worry, Marla," Mom said. "Maybe she will
enroll her dog again someday."

"I hope she does," I replied. "He's a good dog.
They just need to work together a little longer."

46

Sunny and I completed the course and I believe that what the teacher said on the first day of class is true. A trained dog *is* a happy dog.

I think every dog should have his own obedience school diploma!

Now Sunny has many important jobs.

He's a pillow.

He makes sure my brother eats a balanced diet.

He welcomes our guests.

He keeps watch as our family sleeps.

He gives soft fur that my mom spins and knits
into mittens to keep our hands warm.

He does fun tricks. "Sunny, Flip!"

Most of all, Sunny just loves us.

YOUR DOG

A relaxed, cooperative, and obedient dog is a pleasure to live with. Your dog can fit happily into your family's lifestyle.

Many factors go into making your dog who he is. Taking the time to understand your dog will help ensure that your pet becomes a welcome addition to your household.

Each breed has certain characteristics. Although every dog will have his own personality, your dog should look and behave pretty much like the standards set for his breed. If you want a dog who will be happy just keeping you company in a small apartment, a dog with minimal exercise requirements would be a good choice. Many dogs love children, while others tolerate them at best. Like purebreds, mixed breeds carry the genes of their parents.

A puppy begins to learn the day he is born. He develops attitudes and feelings which affect how he will act as a grown dog. A puppy should stay with his mother until he is at least seven weeks old. It is through her that a puppy begins to learn important lessons about life. The mother dog teaches her pups that she is in charge, thus introducing them to leadership acceptance while they are young. She lets them know that they must not bite too hard when playing and that they should not soil their bed.

By the time a puppy leaves his mother, he's already developing a perception of his world and the people in it. The treatment a puppy receives during the developmental period from birth to about twenty weeks plays a very important part in how the animal will react to people and situations throughout his life. A puppy who is shown love and is exposed to different situations within a stable environment has a good chance of growing into a well-adjusted, happy, problem-free dog.

Why train your dog?

Training should begin as soon as you bring your dog home. Show him what he can and cannot do. Teach him the meaning of "No!" Training not only teaches your dog what is expected of him but builds a special bond between dog and handler.

You can train your dog entirely at home, without the benefit of a class situation. However, the advantages of working in a group with a trained instructor are many.

    ℂ Your dog will become comfortable around people and other dogs. He will learn that aggressive behavior is not acceptable.

    ℂ As the handler, you will learn the best ways to communicate your expectations to your dog and to establish a leadership role.

    ℂ The requirements of attending class and completing homework assignments will encourage you to train on a regular basis.

    ℂ Potential problems, both in the dog's behavior and in your training methods, can be detected and corrected by the instructor.

    ℂ Puppy kindergarten classes, designed for dogs as young as eight weeks, offer socialization opportunities and first obedience experiences during an important stage of a puppy's development.

Guidelines For Beginning Obedience Training

1 - DO praise your dog often and with sincerity.

2 - DO play with your dog before and after training. Don't play while working. Let him know that training is serious business.

3 - DO keep the training periods short. Start with five to fifteen minutes twice a day, increasing to thirty minutes. It's better to train for short periods more often than for infrequent long periods of time.

4 - DO be consistent. Always use the same words and signals.

5 - DO make sure your dog understands what you are asking of him.

6 - DO be patient. Not all dogs learn at the same pace.

7 - DO be firm but gentle.

8 - DO end the session with your dog in a happy frame of mind. If you find yourself getting irritated or losing your temper, work briefly on an exercise that you know the dog likes and then discontinue the session. If a dog is given something pleasant to remember, he will eagerly await the next session.

9 - DO seek professional advice when you have questions or concerns.

10 - DON'T tease or make fun of your dog.

11 - DON'T call your dog to punish him for something he has done wrong. Always let good things happen (praise, dinner, etc.) when he comes to you. If you must correct him for unacceptable behavior ("Hey, that pup is chewing my new shoe!"), go to him.

12 - DON'T punish your dog by striking him.

BASIC COMMANDS
YOUR DOG SHOULD LEARN

The following information is presented as an introduction only. Other methods of training may be used by your trainer or local dog training facility. Do not attempt to train your dog using this guide as your only source of information.

Praise: Pet your dog and/or tell him how wonderful he is. "Good dog!"
Release: A word and/or signal which tells your dog that he has completed the exercise, such as "OK" or "All done."

"Heel"

The "heel" exercise, which teaches your dog to walk in a consistent position at your left side, establishes a foundation on which others are built. A dog who has learned to heel will move with you as you walk, rather than pulling, fighting the leash, and possibly tripping you.

1 - Position the dog at your left side, facing the same direction you are. His leash should be slack. His head and shoulder area should be even with your leg.

2 - Say your dog's name and the command "Heel."

3 - Begin walking, leading off with your left leg. A pop on the leash will encourage your dog to move with you. Keep your eyes on the dog at all times and talk to him to keep his attention on you.

4 - If he starts moving out of position, correct him with a quick pop on the leash while repeating the command "Heel."

5 - Always give voice praise after the correction and while the dog is in heel position. "Good dog!"

NOTE: The choke collar, an effective and commonly used training collar, should be used *only* by people who have had instruction in its proper use.

"Sit"

Upon hearing the command "Sit," your dog should instantly assume a sitting position, regardless of what he is doing at the moment. A well-mannered dog, sitting at your side, is one of life's small pleasures!

1 - Position dog at your left side, facing forward.

2 - Tell your dog "Sit" as you pull straight up on his collar with your right hand while pushing down on his hind quarters with your left hand, guiding him into a sitting position.

3 - Praise and release.

If your puppy is very young, or if your dog experiences any discomfort when you push down on his rump, this alternate method may be used.

1 - Position dog at your left side, facing forward.

2 - Tell your dog "Sit" as you pull straight up on his collar with your right hand. At the same time, scoop your left hand under his rump, guiding your dog into a sitting position.

3 - Praise and release.

"Down"

"Down" tells your dog to drop to a lying position. The "down" command puts your dog in a submissive state and is also effective in calming him when necessary.

1 - With dog in sitting position, command "Down."

2 - Place your left foot on the leash and slowly pull up on your end of the leash while repeating "Down." This will encourage your dog into a lying position.

3 - Release tension on the leash when he's down.

4 - Praise and release.

This alternate method is more effective with some dogs.

1 - Place dog in sitting position at your left side.

2 - Kneel down and reach across your dog's shoulders with your left arm, grasping his left front leg with your left hand. Take hold of his right front leg with your right hand.

3 - Command "Down."

4 - Lift his front legs with your hands and lower his body to the ground.

5 - Praise and release.

"Stay"

A dog who has mastered the "stay" command will remain motionless in the position he's asked to take until given further instructions. You'll appreciate your dog's cooperation when you're giving him a bath, grooming him, welcoming guests into your home, or simply getting out of the car.

1 - With your dog sitting at your left side, move your left hand in front of his muzzle and tell him "Stay."

2 - Moving your right foot first, take a step away from your dog.

3 - If your dog moves, say "No," place him back into position and remind him that he's not to move. "Stay."

Watch him so you can correct him while he is *thinking* about moving, rather than after he is already moving.

4 - Your dog should stay in the position you've asked him to take until you *go to him* and release him. "OK!"

"Stand"

The "stand" command can be more clearly defined as a stand-stay, for a dog who has been asked to stand is also expected to stay still until you release him.

A dog who will stand and remain standing is very much appreciated by your veterinarian and groomer, not to mention how much easier you'll find the job of cleaning dirty feet when he comes into the house.

1 - Sit your dog at your left side.

2 - Command "Stand" and pull forward on the collar under your dog's chin with your right hand while lifting your dog's body to a standing position with your left.

3 - Tell him "Stay." He is allowed to move his head and tail, but not his feet.

"Come"

Little can be more frustrating than to call your dog and have him either look at you blankly or ignore you completely as he runs off in the opposite direction. A well-trained dog will come directly to you at your first call. "Come" is the most important command your dog will learn.

1 - While your dog is heeling beside you, say his name and tell him "Come!"

2 - Immediately after giving the command, take three to four steps backward while popping his leash to encourage him to turn around and follow you.

3 - When your dog reaches you, tell him "Sit" and bring him into a straight sit facing you.

4 - Praise and release.

Other books from Woofspun Publishing:

How Nikki Shared Her Coat
"Yes, It's Made from my Dog's Fur"

Available at your bookstore, training center, or pet shop
or request a catalog from:

Woofspun Publishing
P.O. Box 452
Maple Plain, MN   55359-0452
Phone (612) 479-2886   Fax (612) 479-1982